STERLING and the distinctive Sterling logo are registered trademarks of
Sterling Publishing Co., Inc.

Library of Congress Cataloging-in-Publication Data Available

Lot #:
2 4 6 8 10 9 7 5 3 1
12/10
Published by Sterling Publishing Co., Inc.
387 Park Avenue South, New York, NY 10016
TM & © 2011 Paramount Pictures. All Rights Reserved.
Distributed in Canada by Sterling Publishing
c/o Canadian Manda Group, 165 Dufferin Street
Toronto, Ontario, Canada M6K 3H6
Distributed in the United Kingdom by GMC Distribution Services
Castle Place, 166 High Street, Lewes, East Sussex, England BN7 1XU
Distributed in Australia by Capricorn Link (Australia) Pty. Ltd.
P.O. Box 704, Windsor, NSW 2756, Australia

Manufactured in Canada
All rights reserved.

Sterling ISBN 978-1-4027-8442-2

For information about custom editions, special sales, premium and
corporate purchases, please contact Sterling Special Sales
Department at 800-805-5489 or specialsales@sterlingpublishing.com.

THE MOVIE STORYBOOK

By
JUSTINE *and* **RON FONTES**

Based on the screenplay written by
JOHN LOGAN

Story by
JOHN LOGAN,
GORE VERBINSKI,
and **JAMES WARD BYRKIT**

STERLING

New York / London
www.sterlingpublishing.com/kids

"Greetings, Mariachi music lovers! Today we owls sing to celebrate the life and legend of a great Western hero.

"Like many who achieve greatness, this hero had humble beginnings. He started life as an exotic pet, a chameleon in a cage. Four glass walls were his entire world.

"All chameleons can blend into the background. But this chameleon, our hero, was more than a color-changing lizard. He was an actor!"

In his small, glass terrarium "theater," his troupe of actors included a dead bug, a plastic palm tree, and a doll body. Unfortunately, they could hardly be counted on to contribute much to the performance.

"Who am I?" the chameleon mused. "I could be anyone. I could be the sea captain returning from a mighty voyage. Or I could be a rogue anthropologist battling pythons down in the Congo!" he said, fighting his own tail as if it were a giant snake.

No matter how many characters the chameleon made up, he was still alone. He was an actor without an audience.

"What my story needs is an ironic, unexpected event that will propel the hero into conflict," the lizard announced, when suddenly . . .

SCREECH! The chameleon lurched sideways. He and his glass terrarium went flying into the air—right out the window of the station wagon it had been traveling in. It crashed onto the black pavement, shattering all four glass walls.

The chameleon hero watched helplessly as the station wagon rolled away and disappeared down a long, lonely stretch of desert highway.

He blinked one round, lizard eye, and then the other. But the view did not change. The station wagon sped away, shrinking swiftly until it became just a dot on a far-off horizon.

He could hardly believe it. Had he really just been abandoned in the middle of nowhere—doomed to die alone in the desert?

"Oye! Don't be shy. I need a little help here," said a lump on the pavement. It was a squashed armadillo named Roadkill. No matter how many times he got run over, Roadkill never died.

The chameleon was not alone!

"I must get to the other side," explained Roadkill. "This is my quest. The Spirit of the West waits for me. They say he rides in an alabaster carriage."

Thirsty and impatient, the chameleon croaked out, "Water. I need water!"

"If you want to find water, you must first find Dirt," Roadkill replied. "Destiny, she is kind to you. Tomorrow is Wednesday. The water comes. At noon, the townspeople gather for a mysterious ritual."

At the mention of a town, the chameleon perked up.

Roadkill directed, "It's a day's journey. Follow your shadow."

The chameleon was skeptical. "You want me to just walk out into the desert?" he asked.

"We all have our journeys to make," Roadkill replied. "I will see you on the other side."

With nothing but the word of a squashed armadillo to go on, the would-be hero set off across the seemingly endless sands.

The sun beat down mercilessly and baked the chameleon's skin while the hot sand roasted his feet. His only companion was a cactus every few feet and a lumpy, bumpy rock.

Suddenly, the rock shouted, "Don't move! Try to blend in!"

"Blend in? What? Who said that?" the confused chameleon asked, just as an enormous red-tailed hawk soared overhead, looking for a tasty lunch.

The chameleon froze in the shape of a cactus and struggled to blend in, but it was too late! The rock, which wasn't a rock at all, opened an eye. It was a frog named Rock-Eye.

ZOOM! The hawk swooped down. The frog laughed and advised, "Now, you run!"

The chameleon ran for his life, finally scrambling inside an empty bottle where the hawk could not reach him. Exhausted and still thirsty, he crawled into a drainpipe and fell fast asleep.

WHOOSH! Water suddenly gushed from the pipe, shooting the chameleon onto the sand. The pitiless morning sun instantly dried the water before he could drink it.

The chameleon opened his eyes to see the soft, brown leather of a cowboy boot before him. The boot belonged to a rancher lizard named Beans, who was not happy to see him.

"I got a bead on you, stranger," Beans warned. "So get up real slow, unless you want to spend the better part of the afternoon puttin' your face back together! Who are you anyway?"

"Who am I?" the chameleon repeated, unsure what the answer might be.

"I'm asking the questions here!" Beans said firmly. "Our town is drying up, yet someone is dumping water in the desert. What role are you playin' in all of this?"

The chameleon had no idea what she was talking about and chattered on about acting, his favorite pastime, until Beans couldn't take it anymore and drove him into town.

"Town" turned out to be Dirt, a dusty, desolate cluster of ramshackle buildings occupied by a mob of odd-looking critters.

A young mouse named Priscilla threw a rock at the chameleon and warned, "You're a stranger. Strangers don't last long here."

The chameleon tried to blend in by walking and talking like the locals. But they all laughed when he asked for a glass of water.

Buford, the bullfrog behind the counter of Dirt's one and only saloon, handed him a bottle. "Cactus juice. That's what we got," he said.

In Dirt, water was almost too precious to drink. The townsfolk used water as money.

When he drank the fiery juice, the chameleon's eyes nearly rattled out of his head.

A stinky, white-bearded mouse named Spoons stared hard at him. "You're a long way from home. Who exactly are you?"

The chameleon thought for a moment. *Who was he?* Then he looked down at the cactus juice bottle. The label was partially covered by his hand. It said "Rango." Suddenly, he knew his name.

"I'm from the West . . . Out there, beyond the horizon, past the sunset. You might say I'm from everywhere there's trouble brewing," the chameleon said casually. Taking another swig of juice, he concluded, "The name's . . . Rango."

"Hey, are you the fellow that killed the Jenkins brothers?" a cat named Elbows asked.

"With one bullet," Rango bragged.

"All seven brothers?" a bearcat named Elgin asked.

"That's right," Rango replied smoothly. And he began to tell a lie as wide as the Western sky. His tall tales whetted the town's thirst for a hero.

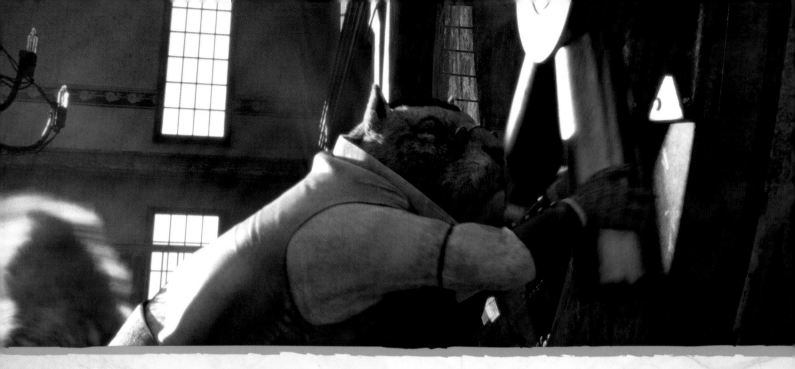

While Rango was busy lying, Beans was at the bank learning a terrible truth. The banker, Mr. Merrimack, showed the pretty-yet-gritty lizard the contents of the vault: a giant jug holding barely a slosh of water.

Beans stared and gasped. "That's all that's left?!"

Beans told Merrimack about the water that dumped Rango in the desert.

The banker couldn't believe it. But he knew the town had suddenly gone dry. "That's why so many people are selling their land."

Merrimack suggested Beans talk to the Mayor. "I hear he's been helping people out in this time of crisis."

Crisis indeed! Someone was controlling the flow of water in Dirt so that every drop would fill his evil pockets. That someone had help from a gang led by a cruel Gila monster known as Bad Bill!

Rango did not mean to start a fight with the bully. The clumsy chameleon just happened to belch fire in Bad Bill's face!

Soon villain and hero faced each other in a showdown in the middle of Main Street. Rango's knees shook so hard his belt fell down around his ankles.

"Alright, now. Listen, I'm going to give you fellas one last chance to reconsider," he said hopefully.

At that moment, a huge hawk flew overhead. The townsfolk ran away. Shutters slammed shut. Even Bad Bill's sidekicks, a rat named Chorizo and two twitchy rabbits named Stump and Kinski, fled in terror.

Unaware that the hawk was right behind him, Rango thought he had scared them all off. "Now that's what I'm talking about. Things are going to be different now that Rango's in town!"

Just as Rango thought he had the situation under control, he turned and saw the horrible hawk! Rango rushed into the outhouse. But the killer bird clawed the flimsy shack right open.

Rango ran all over town in complete panic. But his crazy, klutzy efforts made it look like he was chasing the hawk—instead of the other way around! Finally, the chase was over. Rango had accidentally knocked down the empty water tower on top of the hawk!

Suddenly the clumsy chameleon found himself Sheriff of Dirt! The Mayor himself gave Rango the shiny sheriff's star to wear.

As he strolled proudly down Main Street, Rango noticed the cemetery crowded with the tombstones of previous sheriffs. All of a sudden, he didn't feel so happy about being put in charge.

"Can I have your boots when you're dead?" Priscilla asked Rango. The idea didn't make him feel one bit better about the job.

On Wednesday, the entire town gathered for their weekly flow of water, which came from a pipe sticking out of the ground.

Rango couldn't wait for his first sip of water. But the only thing that trickled out of the giant faucet was mud!

To make matters worse, the town bank had been robbed. Someone had tunneled into the vault and stolen all of the townsfolks' water savings.

Everyone looked to Sheriff Rango to track down the varmints.

Rango formed a posse, and they all headed down into the hole in the middle of the street.

Little Priscilla fretted, "Sheriff, you are going to bring that water back, aren't you?"

"Count on it, little sister," Rango promised as he dropped down the hole.

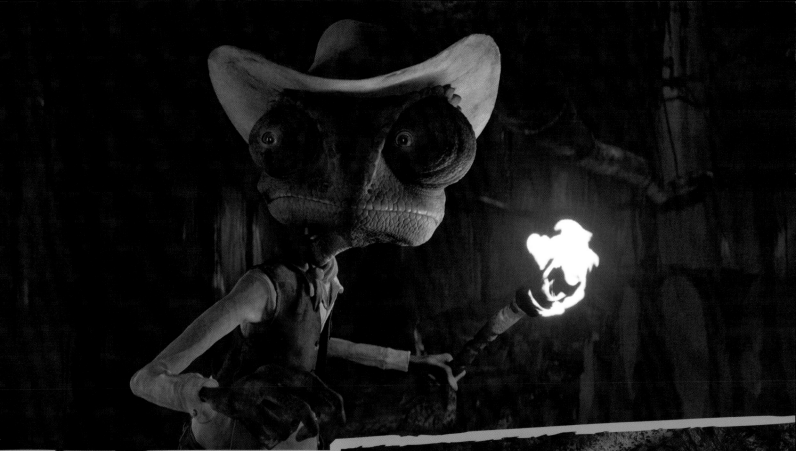

The posse discovered a huge network of tunnels beneath Dirt. They wondered which way they should go when someone spotted an old water pipe.

They followed the pipe to what seemed like a dead end. Sheriff Rango commanded, "Snuff out them torches."

In the resulting blackness, the posse suddenly saw a sliver of light above them. Thick roots twisted toward the light.

The posse climbed the roots. Finally above ground, the group
found themselves in a field—and poor Mr. Merrimack, the banker.
Mr. Merrimack had been drowned! But how could he have been
drowned when there was no water?

Muddy boot prints put the posse on a fresh trail.

"Now . . . WE RIDE!" Rango exclaimed.

The posse galloped atop roadrunners until the sun sank below
the horizon.

Around a blazing campfire, Rango entertained them with tales of the Spirit of the West. But nobody could relax. Even with the hawk gone and the lack of water, there was still a third danger to worry about: Rattlesnake Jake. Rattlesnake Jake wore a black cowboy hat and terrified everyone to bits.

Rango bragged, "I'm not scared of Jake. He's my brother. Why, I used to pour his venom in my coffee just to give it tang."

While the others slept, Beans and Rango looked up at the night's bright stars. Rango shuddered at the chilly air—and the eerie, desert landscape.

"Do you ever feel like the cactus is looking at you?" he asked.

Beans replied, "Folks call those the 'Walking Cactus.' There's an old legend that they actually walk across the desert to find water."

Beans didn't really believe the legend, but she wanted to believe in Rango.

"We'll find the water. I promise," he assured her.

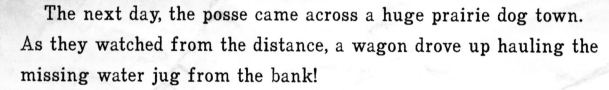

The next day, the posse came across a huge prairie dog town.
As they watched from the distance, a wagon drove up hauling the
missing water jug from the bank!

Sheriff Rango planned a special ambush. He borrowed Beans' dress
and disguised himself as a girl. The posse pretended to be a traveling
theatre troupe. They put on a play for the prairie dogs. In the middle
of the performance, the posse attacked!

Rango told Pappy, the prairie dog leader, "We got you surrounded.
So you and your entire family get your hands up."

The old dog laughed. "My entire family?"

Suddenly, the ground boiled with hundreds of rodents.

Rango screamed, "RUNNNNN!"

"Get on the wagon!" Beans added, as the panicked posse fled the buck-toothed, bloodthirsty horde.

The wagon raced through the canyon. Then just when the posse thought they were safe, a hooting, hollering cloud emerged from the cliffs.

With a great flapping of wings and RATTA-TAT-TAT, prairie dogs riding bats hunted down the retreating posse.

Rango's wagon hit a boulder and crashed, breaking the giant jug. Both sides of the fight stared, stunned to discover that the bottle was empty!

Pappy gasped. "No water?! What are we fightin' for?"

When Rango tried to arrest Pappy, one of his sons objected. Ezekiel said, "We didn't have anything to do with Mr. Merrimack. We tunneled into that vault, but there was nothing in it. We found the jug in the desert."

Jedidiah added, "Somebody robbed the bank before we robbed it."

Beans looked at Rango, but the sheriff had no answers. Finally, he decided to bring the prairie dogs to Dirt to sort the whole thing out.

Thirsty and suspicious, Rango paid a visit to the Mayor. Certain things the old tortoise had said just didn't add up.

The Mayor was playing golf with Bad Bill and his gang at a construction site.

Rango accused the Mayor of masterminding the water drought. "You said 'control the water and you control everything,'" Rango said.

The Mayor sank a perfect putt before replying, "How on earth could I possibly control the water?"

Rango didn't know—yet. So he asked about Mr. Merrimack.

The Mayor answered, "Careful, Mr. Rango. You seem to forget that you're just one little lizard."

"You seem to forget I'm the law around these parts," Rango replied.

As soon as Rango was out of earshot, the Mayor instructed Bad Bill to call for backup: Rattlesnake Jake!

Even Bad Bill quaked at the mention of the snake's name.

But the Mayor insisted, "Do it!"

As Rattlesnake Jake slithered toward Dirt, the angry mob grumbled outside the jail. They were frustrated. Without water, they would lose their land. Without water, they would never survive the harsh Mojave Desert.

Buford explained, "We got no hope without that water."

"We got nothing left to believe in," added Spoons.

Rango pointed to the sheriff sign. "As long as that sign says 'Sheriff,' you can believe that there's law and order in this town. Believe in me. Believe in that sign. As long as it hangs there, we got hope."

Then, without warning, the sign fell down into the dust. And everyone heard . . .

. . . the loud, terrifying
rattle of Rattlesnake Jake's tail.

The crowd stepped away from the huge snake as Jake called, "Hello,
brother!" He drained some venom into a cup and hissed, "Thirsssty?"

The skinny chameleon twitched in terror.

Jake sneered, "Thessse good folks believe your ssstoriesss. They
think you're going to sssave their little town. But you're not who you
sssay you are. You're not even from the Wessst, are you?"

"No," Rango admitted softly.

Jake continued, "Lisssten clossse, you fraud. Thisss isss my town
now. Don't ever let me sssee you again."

Embarrassed and afraid, Rango walked away—and just kept walking. He walked into the desert until he found his wind-up fish, Mr. Timms, and his doll. He put his arm around his old friend, and sighed. "Who am I? I am nobody."

With nowhere else to go, Rango crossed the highway. On the other side, he saw a gleaming golf cart and a tall, lean man with a flat hat. It was the Spirit of the West!

"It doesn't matter what they call you," advised the Spirit of the West. "It's the deeds that make the man."

Rango sighed. "My deeds just made things worse. My friends need a real hero."

"Then be a hero," the Spirit said. "No man can walk out on his own story."

Rango turned and saw Roadkill. The armadillo had finally made it to the other side. He showed Rango one cactus, and then two, and then more—all slowly walking toward big pipes, fountains, and the shining buildings of . . . Las Vegas!

Rango followed a cactus to a huge water valve surrounded by muddy boot prints. The pipe had an emergency shut-off switch on it. Suddenly everything made sense. For the first time in his life, Rango knew what to do!

First, Rango went to the prairie dog town. Then he returned to Dirt and put on his sheriff's badge. Rango had help—and a plan!

In the middle of the dusty street, Rango shouted, "JAAAKE! I'M CALLING YOU OUT!"

When Rattlesnake Jake slithered out, Rango asked, "Thirsty, brother?"

WHOOSH! Geysers erupted all over Dirt. One was right under Rattlesnake Jake! The prairie dogs released all the water the Mayor had been hoarding.

A swarm of bats swooped down. The prairie dogs attacked
Rattlesnake Jake. The Mayor tried to use Beans as a hostage, but
Rango freed her. Everything was happening at once.

In the end, Jake ended up getting rid of the real bad guy, the
Mayor. As he slithered out of Dirt, the snake said, "I tip my hat
to you, Rango. From one legend to another."

That is the story of how Sheriff Rango saved the town of Dirt.

Little Priscilla hugged her champion. "Rango! You brought back the water, just like you promised! You really are a hero."

Everyone in town splashed and played, sipped, slurped, and swam in the cool, refreshing water. Rango had saved the day—with a little help from a lot of friends.

After that great day, the town changed forever. Water was no longer used as money. Folks took baths, instead of just staying dirty. And even the town's name was changed from Dirt to Mud.

It was practically paradise. And yet . . .

Rango wanted to leave. He was needed elsewhere.

"There's trouble down in Dry Creek," Rango explained. "Bad Bill's been acting up again."

Beans fretted. "You come back with all your digits. Don't go trying to be a hero."

Rango sighed. Being a hero had become his life.

Priscilla understood. A hero has to do what a hero has to do: risk his life saving towns and defending justice.

Rango and Beans said their goodbyes. It was time for Rango to ride again. The once-cowardly chameleon was no longer a lizard without an identity. He was Rango! His legend would live as long as there were sunsets, villains, varmints, and townsfolk who needed someone to believe in.

True to form, Rango almost fell off his roadrunner as he galloped away from town. Clumsily, he managed to stay in the saddle, and rode off toward the amber sunset and his next wild adventure.

★ BEHIND THE SCENES ★

The amazing art and life-like animation for *Rango* was not made overnight. It took artists and illustrators months to perfect every last detail of the characters. Before making it to the big screen, the talented team at Industrial Light and Magic created hundreds of character and set sketches, sculptures, and paintings for inspiration and research. Their animation experts then took that hand-drawn artwork and used it as a basis for the final CGI (computer-generated imagery) animation you see in theaters. Here is some "behind-the-scenes" art that shows how *Rango* came to life.

Sketch of the prairie dog hideout

Sketch of Rango

Sketch of Rango in the saloon

Sketch of Dirt

Painting of Rattlesnake Jake

Sketch of the underground tunnel

Painting of the water tower

Painting of the sheriff graveyard